Gertrude Chandler Warner's

THE BOXCAR CHILDREN
GRAPHIC NOVELS

THE AMUSEMENT PARK MYSTERY

When the Aldens visit their cousins, they're in for a surprise—there's an amusement park nearby! It has everything they could ask for, with plenty of rides and games. But the children see strange lights coming from the closed park at night. And then a mysterious phone call warns them to stay away! Just what is going on at the amusement park?

THE BOXCAR CHILDREN
GRAPHIC NOVELS

Gertrude Chandler Warner's

THE BOXCAR CHILDREN
THE AMUSEMENT PARK MYSTERY

Adapted by Shannon Eric Denton
Illustrated by Mike Dubisch

Henry Alden

Watch

Jessie Alden

Violet Alden

Benny Alden

Adapted by Shannon Eric Denton
Illustrated by Mike Dubisch
Colored by Carlos Badilla
Lettered by Johnny Lowe
Edited by Stephanie Hedlund
Interior layout and design by Kristen Fitzner Denton
Cover art by Mike Dubisch
Book design and packaging by Shannon Eric Denton

Library of Congress Cataloging-in-Publication Data
is available from the Library of Congress.

10 9 8 7 6 5 4 3 2 1 LB 14 13 12 11 10 09

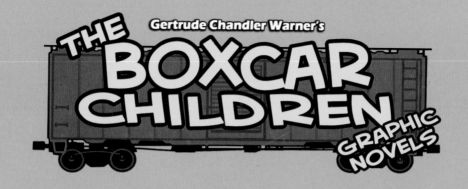

Gertrude Chandler Warner's

THE BOXCAR CHILDREN

Graphic Novels

THE AMUSEMENT PARK MYSTERY

Contents

Henry, Jessie, Violet, and Benny Alden were visiting their cousin Joe and his wife, Alice.

I can't wait to go to the amusement park that's near Joe and Alice's house.

Where are Joe and Alice?

Oh, they'll be here. They're always on time.

Alice is working at the museum, but she'll be home for dinner. Welcome to Pine Grove.

Cousin Joe picked the Aldens up from the train station and drove through town on the way home.

The children were staying in Joe and Alice's guesthouse. They were excited for the next day.

Wait until you see the beautiful merry-go-round at the amusement park. The horses are very old and valuable.

I can't wait to see them.

I can't wait to ride them!

The next morning, the kids rode bikes to the amusement park. Benny talked everyone into having cotton candy for breakfast.

Welcome to Pine Grove. I'm Frank Arnold and this is my wife, Sheila.

And I'm Henry Alden.

We serve hamburgers and hot dogs, too. Come back for lunch!

At the merry-go-round...

I've never seen such beautiful horses.

They're all so beautiful.

The children played and ate all morning.

By midafternoon the children were tired.

I'm ready to go home.

Me too. I was ready after that scary Ferris wheel.

Even though the Aldens were tired, it had been a wonderful day.

Their cousins were friends with Joshua Eaton and his daughter, Karen. Mr. Eaton owned the amusement park! They all had dinner together that night.

How did you all like my amusement park?

I loved the merry-go-round horses.

You see, dear. We must keep our valuable carousel.

Who cares about some dumb wooden horses? We have to modernize. We'll just see which will get more use--the new House of Mirrors or the old merry-go-round.

With the money we'd earn from selling the horses to collectors, we could install new rides. You have to get with the times, Dad.

As long as I'm around, the horses will be too.

A few days later, the Aldens were going for a swim in the nearby lake. On the way, they overheard someone talking on the beach!

CLEAR LAKE

But each horse is worth a fortune.

PETER MCKENZIE

If it were up to me, I'd get rid of the carousel. We could sell those horses and make a lot of money. But my father...

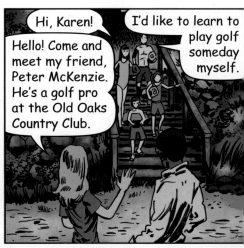

Hi, Karen!

Hello! Come and meet my friend, Peter McKenzie. He's a golf pro at the Old Oaks Country Club.

I'd like to learn to play golf someday myself.

If you want a lesson, look me up.

Let's go, Peter.

I want to check the House of Mirrors.

The children soon forgot about Karen. They played all morning at the lake and looked forward to their afternoon at the amusement park.

The kids ate more cotton candy and rode the tilt-a-whirl before heading back to the merry-go-round. Jessie was first to notice Peter sketching the horses.

Hello, Jessie and Violet.

SLAM!

I've got to go. I-I'm late.

ENTRANCE ▷

Why do you suppose Peter acted as if he had a secret?

I don't know, it's a mystery!

Next, the kids gave the Hall of Mirrors a try. After almost losing Jessie inside, they decided to head back to the merry-go-round for one last ride...

Everyone enjoyed the merry-go-round but Benny, whose horse didn't move up or down.

Then, they swung on the swings...

I like the merry-go-round better.

So, the Aldens rode the merry-go-round again...

I want the dapple gray. He's my favorite.

At dinner that night...

What rides did you go on today, Benny?

The tilt-a-whirl and the swings. But I like the merry-go-round the best, even though the dapple gray had a big scratch on its side.

A scratch...I wonder how it got there!

The next morning, the kids set out to tell Joshua Eaton about the problems with the merry-go-round.

I wonder if someone was purposely hurting the merry-go-round horses...

We're not open!

We need to see Mr. Eaton. Could you tell us where he is?

He's back in the trailer.

Mr. Eaton, may we speak with you?

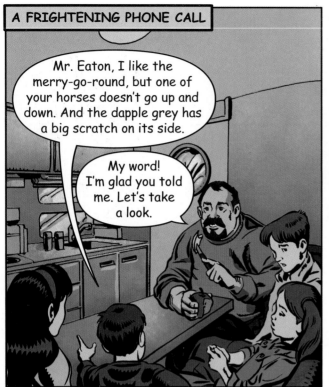

Mr. Eaton, I like the merry-go-round, but one of your horses doesn't go up and down. And the dapple grey has a big scratch on its side.

My word! I'm glad you told me. Let's take a look.

One horse doesn't go up and down, and suddenly there's a big scratch on another one. It's strange.

We'll help you find who did this!

That horse's stomach doesn't have any paint on it. It's all bare wood!

This is terrible!

After their trip to the amusement park, the children biked home. They were eager to forget about the problems with the horses, but couldn't.

RINNNGGG

14

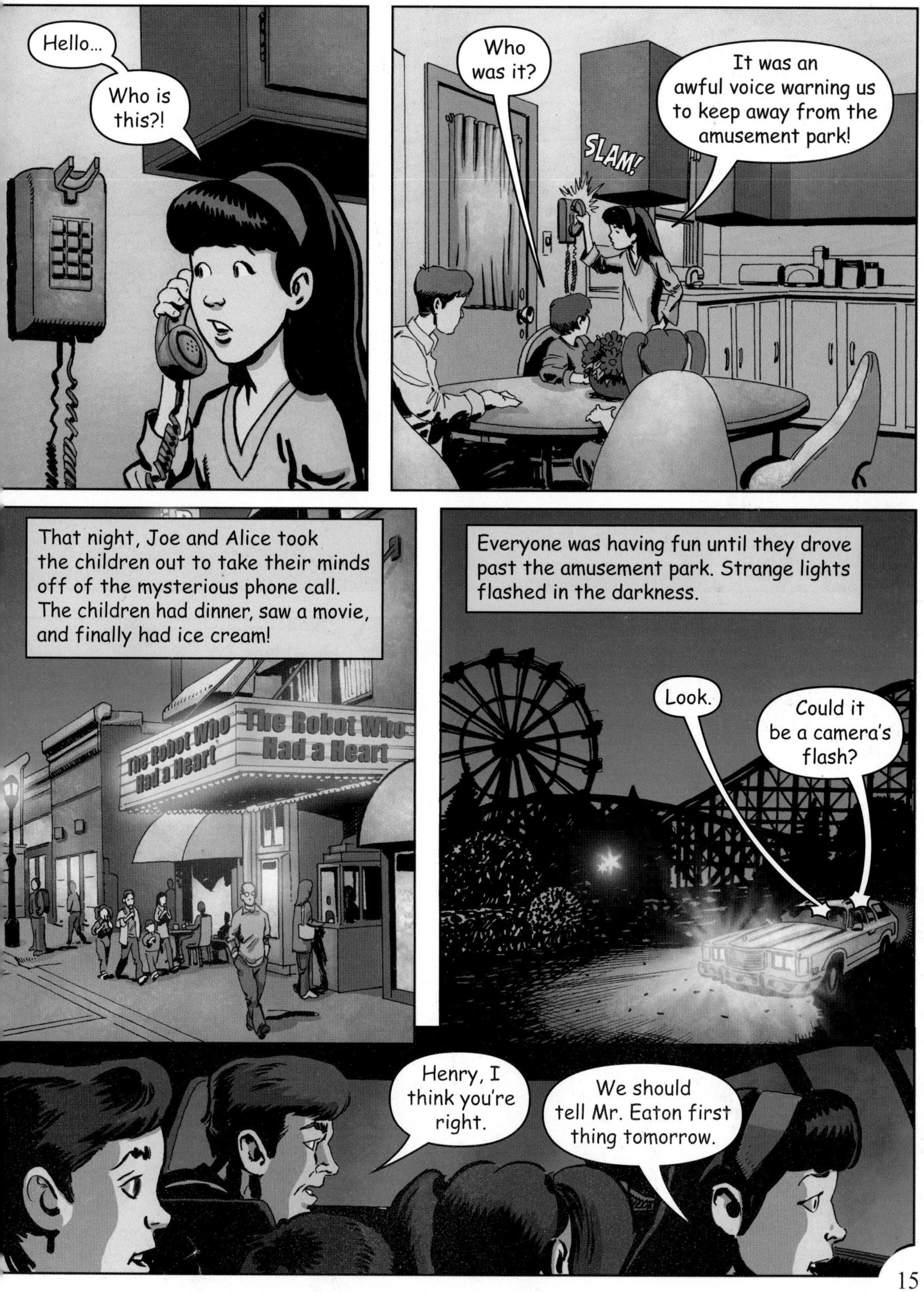
Hello...
Who is this?!
Who was it?
It was an awful voice warning us to keep away from the amusement park!
SLAM!
That night, Joe and Alice took the children out to take their minds off of the mysterious phone call. The children had dinner, saw a movie, and finally had ice cream!
The Robot Who Had a Heart
The Robot Who Had a Heart
Everyone was having fun until they drove past the amusement park. Strange lights flashed in the darkness.
Look.
Could it be a camera's flash?
Henry, I think you're right.
We should tell Mr. Eaton first thing tomorrow.

The Alden children went back to their guesthouse, but the strange flashing lights were still on everyone's minds.

I wish I knew what was going on.

I don't want anything to happen to my beautiful horses.

None of us do. But look at all the strange things that have happened around the merry-go-round.

Someone's sneaking in the park at night to take pictures and to hurt the horses.

This is getting weirder and weirder.

We'll go to the park tomorrow. Joshua will be able to shed some light on what's going on.

The next morning, the Aldens rode their bicycles to the amusement park to tell Mr. Eaton about what they'd seen.

Should we tell Mr. Eaton about your phone call?

He has enough to worry about. Let's keep the call our little secret.

Hi, Aldens. Do you want a free ride before we open the park?

Thanks, but not today, Mr. Eaton. We need to talk to you.

Okay, come over and have a seat.

Last night, when we drove by the closed park we saw flashing lights.

We think someone might have been taking pictures.

Hi, Dad. Hello, Aldens.

Hello.

Karen, the children told me that someone was taking pictures here last night.

And three of my horses have been tampered with!

Three?

Yes, three! The light gray doesn't go up and down. The dapple gray has a big scratch. And the chocolate brown's stomach isn't painted!

Is that so? It doesn't sound too serious to me.

It's serious! The horses are being hurt.

This morning I carefully examined all the horses. Now I'm wondering if they might not be fakes!

Fakes! I doubt that.

There are experts who would know if these were real. I have to find someone to examine my horses!

You're not going to call the police are you? That wouldn't be good for the park.

17

The next day, the children received another warning from the mysterious caller.

Who is this?

Henry, these calls scare me.

Let's go back to the park and see what's happening.

CLICK

I'm ready.

The children raced back to the park. They discovered a woman examining the horses on the carousel.

Hi, Aldens. This is Ms. Margaret Macy, an expert. Frank told me about her and we were lucky to get her before she left town.

You don't have to worry, Mr. Eaton. These horses are definitely the originals.

I can't thank you enough. You've made me very happy.

I'm glad Ms. Macy happened to be near here and could come right away.

The children were happy until they went home to find a letter addressed to them! Jessie read it aloud...

"Aldens, go home! You're snoopy and don't belong here! Don't return to the amusement park. Signed, The Watcher."

I say **we** become the watchers.

Yes, Benny. We won't let a few phone calls and a letter keep us from going to the park. We'll keep this to ourselves for now though.

THE TERRIBLE FERRIS WHEEL RIDE

Look, there's Sheila and Frank-- the people who run the snack bar at the amusement park.

Before heading back to the park, the children stopped at Lou's drugstore for some chocolate sodas.

Where?

They're with Margaret Macy! Wasn't Frank the one who told Mr. Eaton that she was in town and an expert?

Oh, Sheila's handing Ms. Macy an envelope.

Henry soon realized that Frank was paying Ms. Macy for pretending to be an expert, examining Mr. Eaton's horses, and saying they were real.

As Sheila, Frank, and Ms. Macy left the drugstore, Sheila spotted the Aldens. The children knew they had to hurry and get to the park to warn Mr. Eaton.

Moments later...

Let's not find Mr. Eaton right away. We don't want Frank and Sheila watching us.

You're right, Violet. Why don't we ride the Ferris wheel?

It's too tall.

Exactly! That way we'll be able to see the whole park and keep an eye on Frank and Sheila.

Soon they were seated on the Ferris wheel, going up, up in the air.

I'm afraid to look down when we're at the top. But, we can't be good detectives if we can't see what's going on.

I like to see everything. Hey, I can see Sheila below!

Sheila had tricked the ride operator into taking a break and letting her operate the controls! She shut off the ride with the Aldens trapped at the top!

We're the only ones on the Ferris wheel!

I know!

I don't like this ride!

Will we ever get down?

Sure we will.

LET US DOWN!

It was Frank who finally let them down.

Sheila! That's enough!

I don't like the Ferris wheel!

It will be a long time before I ride it again, too.

The ride was over...

We're fine.

Just a little wobbly.

Thank heavens you're safe!

Sheila, what were you doing? What's going on?

Sheila and Frank had some explaining to do...

We stole three of the horses. I went along with the plan for the money, but when I saw the children at the top of the Ferris wheel, I changed my mind. When it comes to hurting little kids, I draw the line.

Thanks to the Aldens, we knew about the three damaged horses...but we didn't know YOU were guilty. Where are my horses?

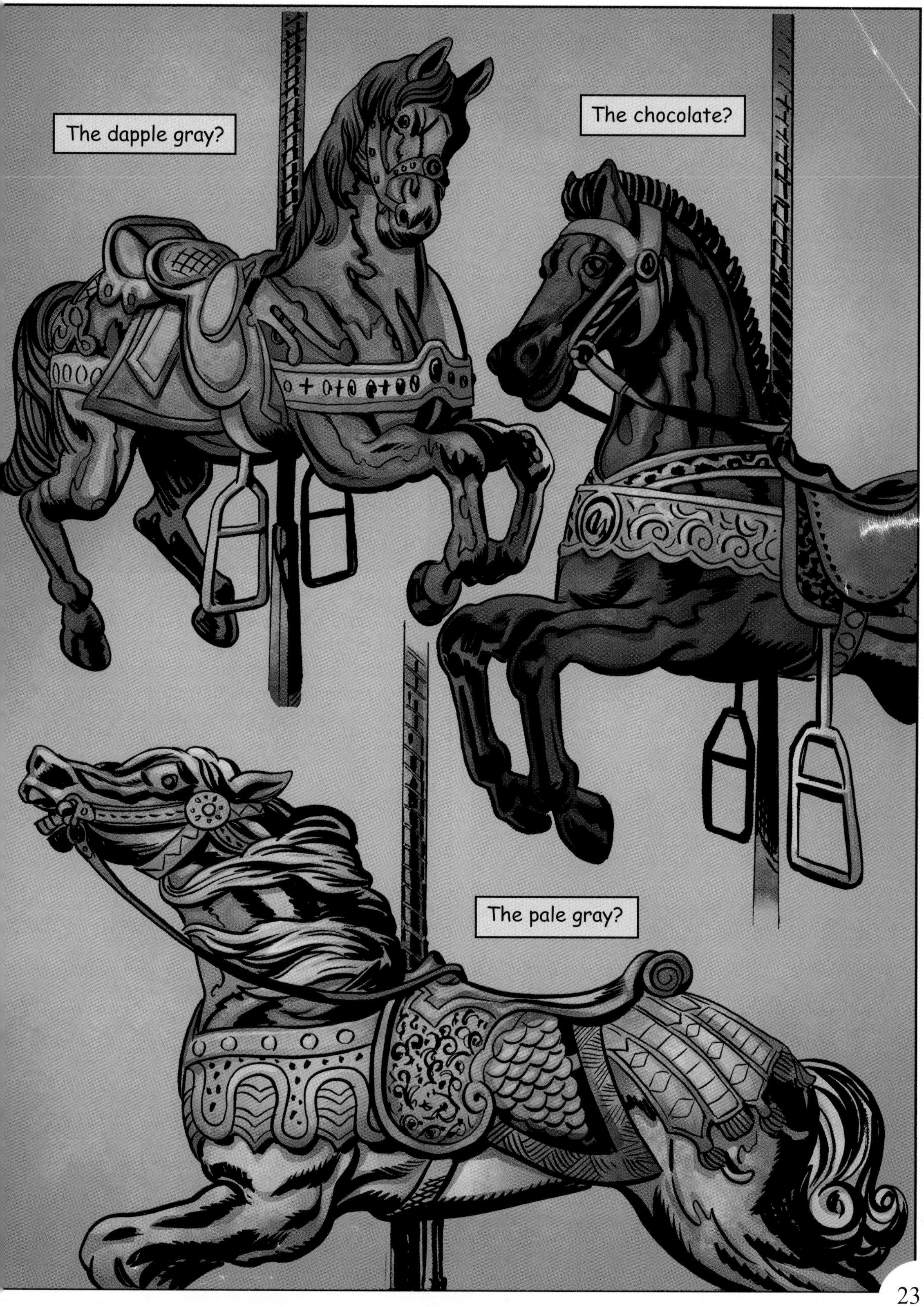
The dapple gray?
The chocolate?
The pale gray?

Frank explained that they had clever artists copy the real horses from pictures.

When the carvers finished, they painted the fake horses just like the originals.

Except they forgot to paint one horse's stomach!

Everything was done at night. When the fake horses were ready, we substituted them for the originals. We were going to be rich. But you kids noticed every mistake.

If it hadn't been for these kids we would have been rich! You were always around the merry-go-round, no matter what I did.

Take it easy, Sheila.

After the fake horses were in place, a truck hauled the original horses to the barn. Our biggest mistake was when we paid Margaret Macy in broad daylight. You kids even saw that!

Stop!

She's getting away!

Benny took off after Sheila.

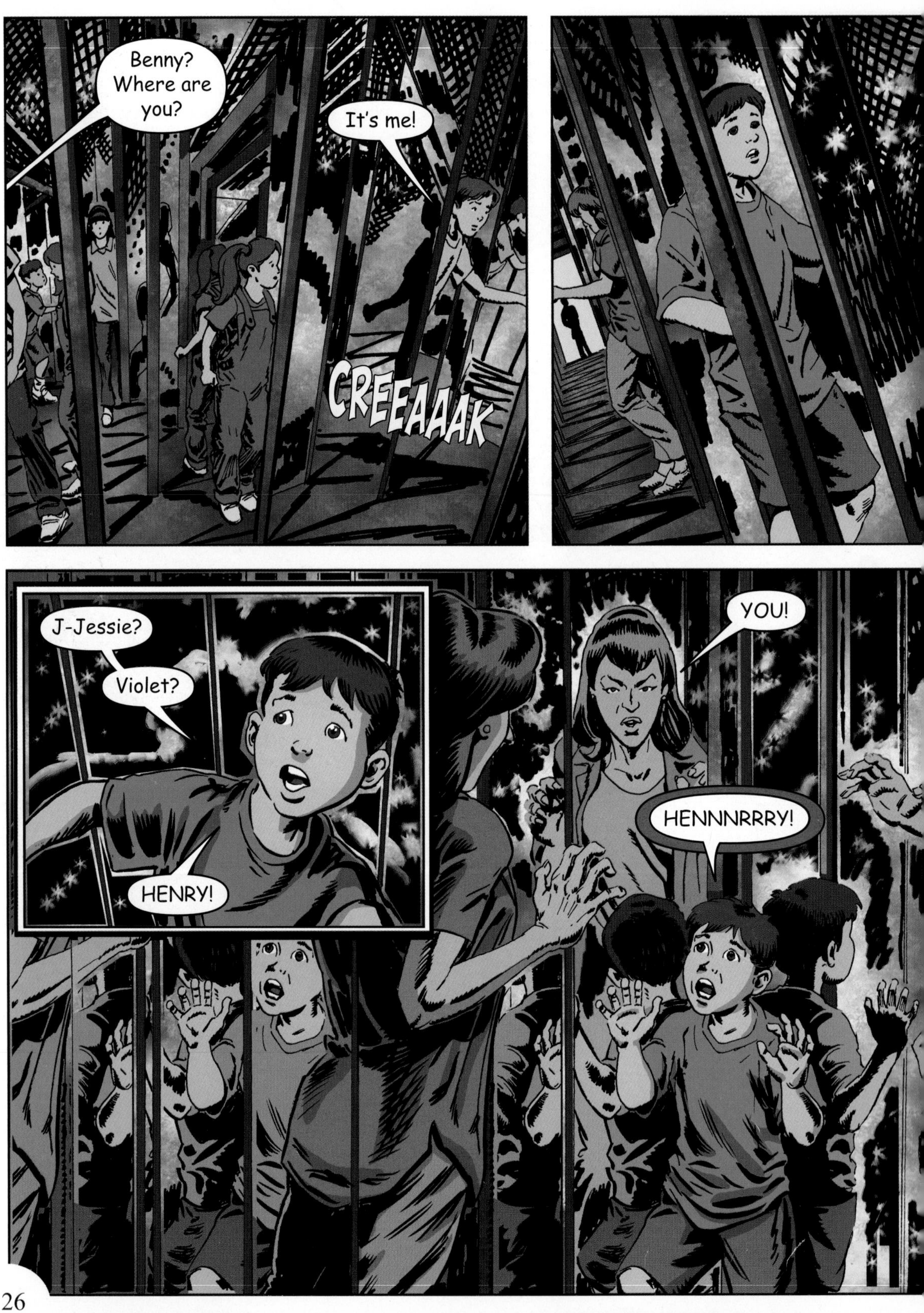

Benny? Where are you?
It's me!
CREEAAAK
J-Jessie?
Violet?
HENRY!
YOU!
HENNNRRRY!

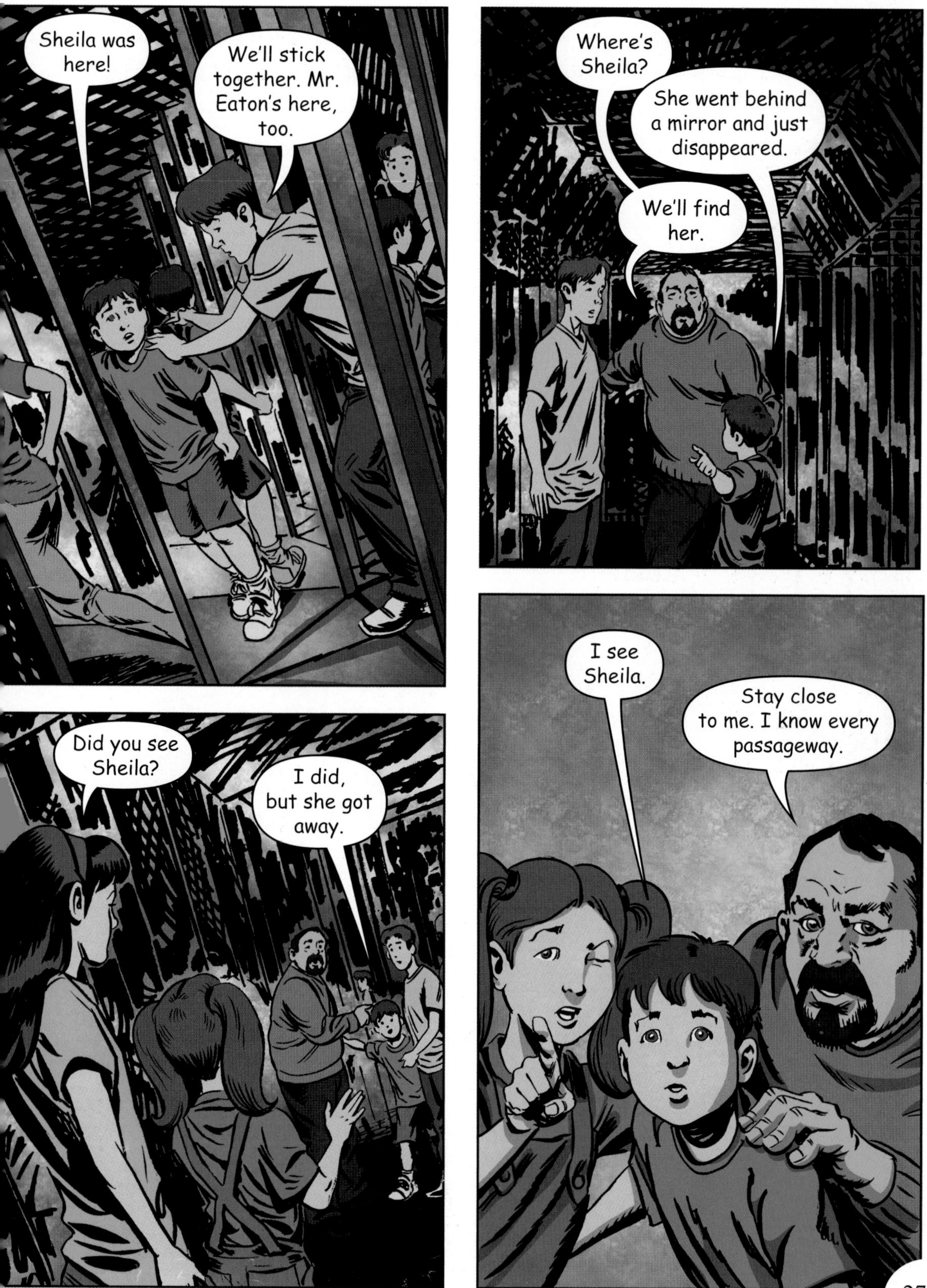
Sheila was here!
We'll stick together. Mr. Eaton's here, too.
Where's Sheila?
She went behind a mirror and just disappeared.
We'll find her.
Did you see Sheila?
I did, but she got away.
I see Sheila.
Stay close to me. I know every passageway.

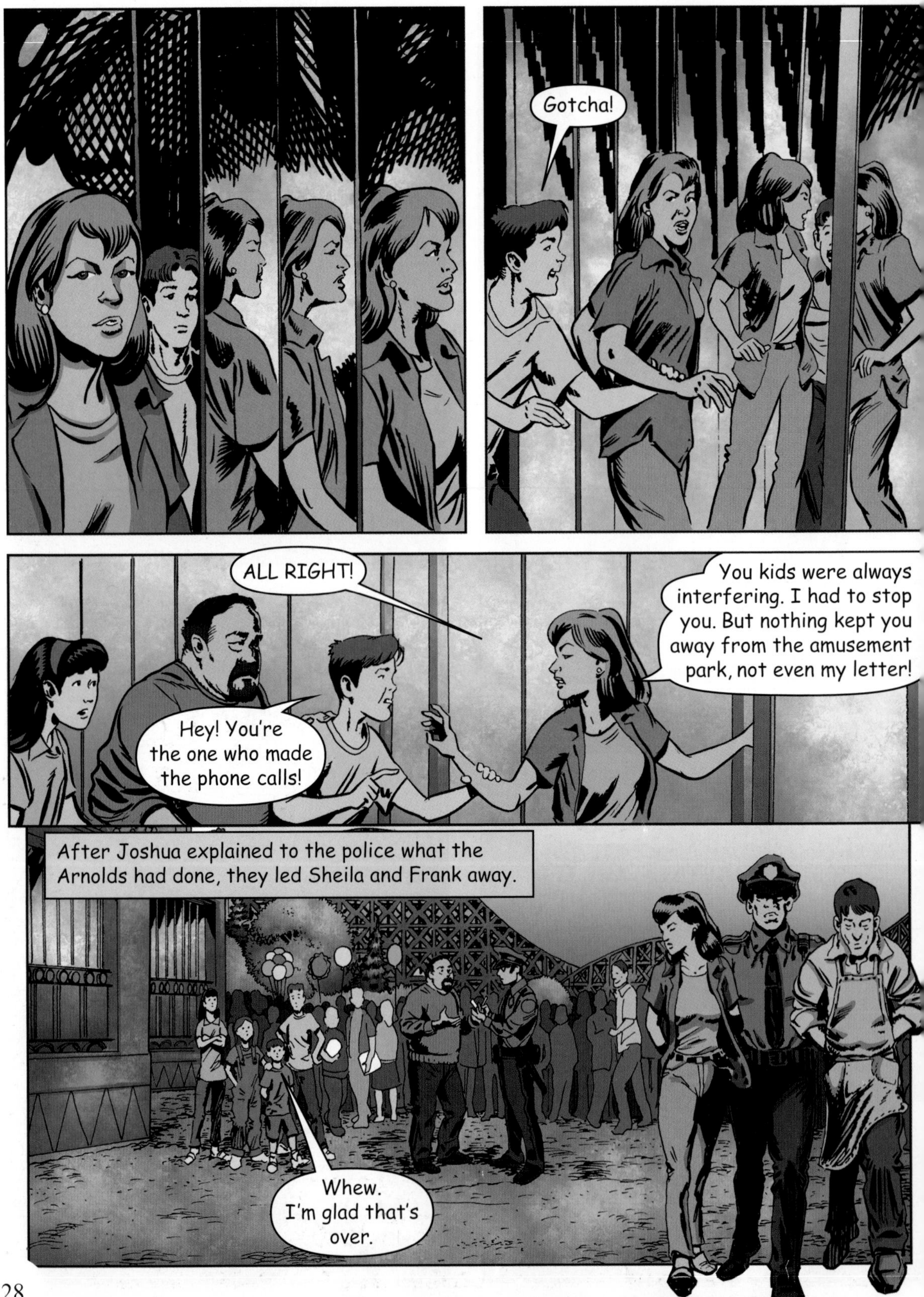
Gotcha!
ALL RIGHT!
You kids were always interfering. I had to stop you. But nothing kept you away from the amusement park, not even my letter!
Hey! You're the one who made the phone calls!
After Joshua explained to the police what the Arnolds had done, they led Sheila and Frank away.
Whew. I'm glad that's over.

Dad, I'm sorry I wanted to get rid of the merry-go-round. Ned told me about the thieves. I didn't realize how important it was to you.

You'll keep the merry-go-round?

Yes, Benny. The carousel will be the main attraction. A roller coaster would take up too much space! I'll never complain about the horses again.

You don't know how much this means to me, dear.

Let's go and get the horses.

We'll need a truck.

I'll call Peter to get one. Everyone can go. If it hadn't been for the Aldens, we wouldn't have discovered the three fake horses.

PINE GROVE AMUSEMENT PARK THANKS
COME AGAIN SOON

Yes indeed, the children are invited.

Peter picked everyone up in his work truck and soon they were all out at the old barn.

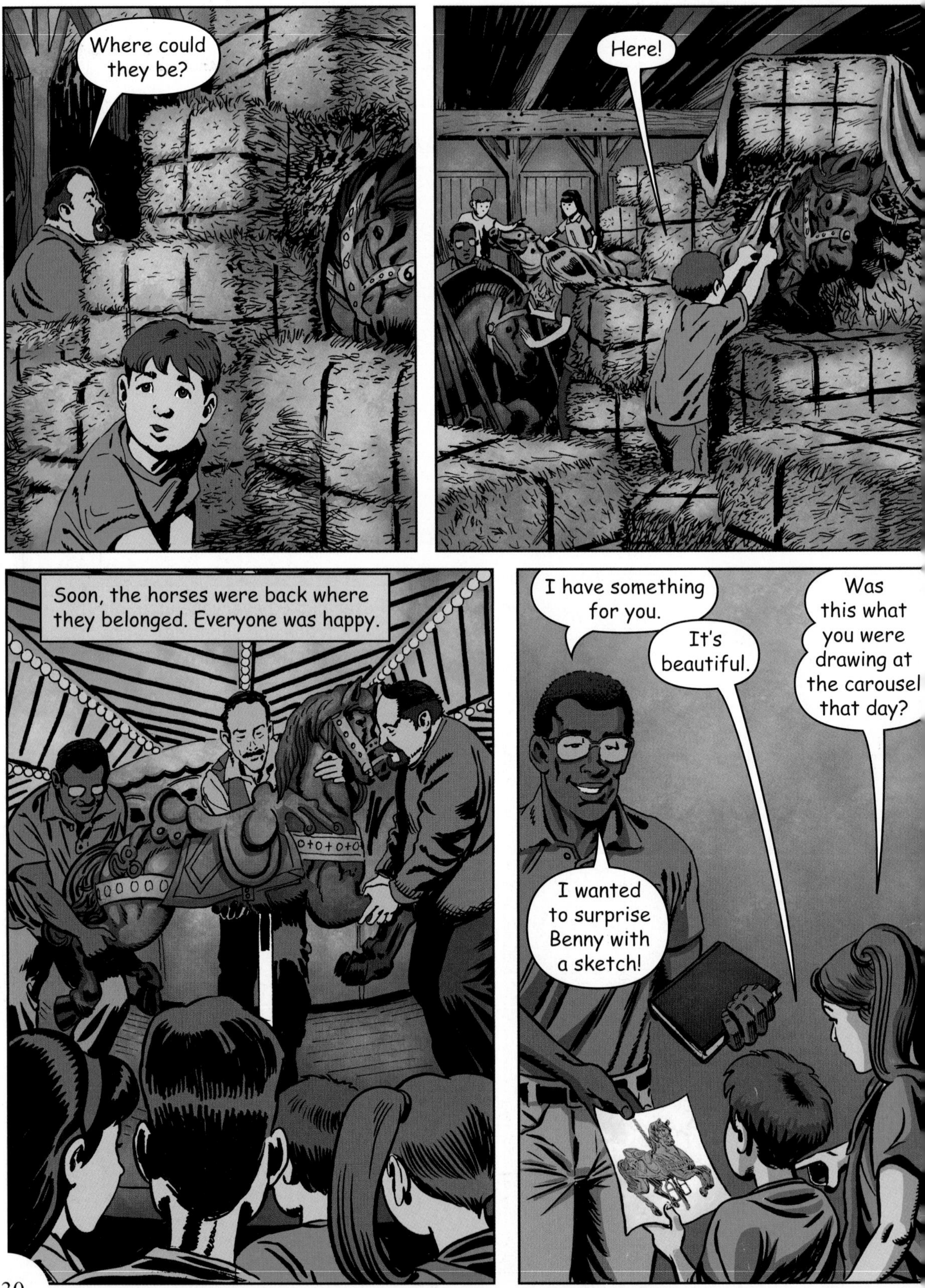
Where could they be?
Here!
Soon, the horses were back where they belonged. Everyone was happy.
I have something for you.
It's beautiful.
Was this what you were drawing at the carousel that day?
I wanted to surprise Benny with a sketch!

Happily the Aldens returned to Joe and Alice's house and prepared to return home. They were proud they had helped Mr. Eaton find his beautiful horses.

Benny couldn't wait to tell Grandfather the whole story.

ABOUT THE CREATOR

Gertrude Chandler Warner was born on April 16, 1890, in Putnam, Connecticut. In 1918, Warner began teaching at Israel Putnam School. As a teacher, she discovered that many readers who liked an exciting story could not find books that were both easy and fun to read. She decided to try to meet this need. In 1942, *The Boxcar Children* was published for these readers.

Warner drew on her own experience to write *The Boxcar Children*. As a child she spent hours watching trains go by on the tracks near her family home. She often dreamed about what it would be like to live in a caboose or freight car—just as the Alden children do.

When readers asked for more Alden adventures, Warner began additional stories. While the mystery element is central to each of the books, she never thought of them as strictly juvenile mysteries. She liked to stress the Aldens' independence. Henry, Jessie, Violet, and Benny go about most of their adventures with as little adult supervision as possible—something that delights young readers.

During her lifetime, Warner received hundreds of letters from fans as she continued the Aldens' adventures, writing nineteen Boxcar Children books in all. After her death in 1979, her publisher, Albert Whitman and Company, carried on Warner's vision. Today, the Boxcar Children series has more than 100 books.